WHAT THE WITCH LEFT

by RUTH CHEW

illustrated by the author

SCHOLASTIC INC.
New York Toronto London Auckland Sydney

Reading level is determined by using
the Spache Readability Formula.
2.2 signifies high 2nd-grade level.

ISBN 0-590-33944-3

12 11 10 9 8 7 6 5 4 3 2   6 7 8 9/8 0/9

Printed in the U.S.A.   11

To
David Silver

CHAPTER ONE

"WHAT do you keep in here, Katy?"
Louise walked over to the tall chest of
drawers in the corner of Katy's room.
The chest was dark and old and covered
with scratches.

Katy put down the black jelly bean
she was using for an eyebrow pencil.
"I'm not supposed to touch the stuff in
that chest. My mother stores things in it."

Louise pulled open the top drawer.
The smell of mothballs filled the air.
"Isn't that the sweater you wore last year,
Katy? And here's your tweed skirt."

Katy shut the drawer. "They're too small for me," she said. "And I told you Mother doesn't want me going into the chest. Do you want to get me into trouble?"

Louise looked out of the window at the pouring rain. "I'm bored," she said, "and I'm your guest, Katy. It's your duty to amuse me." She opened the second drawer. It was filled with old sheets and blankets. "It won't hurt to *look* at the things," Louise said, "not that they're all that interesting."

The third drawer held a lot of old handbags. "I sometimes play with those," Katy admitted, "but I always put them back just the way they were, so Mother won't notice."

The bottom drawer was locked. "The stuff in there belongs to Aunt Martha," Katy said. "She left it here ages ago when she went on a trip."

"Where's the key to the drawer?" Louise wanted to know.

"I think Mother hid it in her night table," Katy said. "I found a key there one day when I was looking for some Scotch tape."

"Your mother isn't home," Louise said.

Katy grinned. She ran out of the room and came back a few moments later with a little key. It was worn and old, but it fitted into the lock of the bottom drawer and turned easily.

Katy opened the drawer. Louise reached in and took out a little round mirror with a curly handle and a tarnished silver frame.

"We have to remember exactly how the things fit in," Katy said.

"Of course." Louise put the mirror on the floor and lifted a pile of cloth out of the drawer. When she shook it, the cloth unfolded. It was a long bathrobe with a big floppy hood. The cloth was worn thin in places, but it was still brightly colored in a strange pattern.

"Great for playing Arabs," Louise said.

"We're only going to *look* at the things, not play with them," Katy reminded her. She saw something that looked like a rolled-up pair of faded nylon stockings. "I wonder why Aunt Martha would leave these here." She picked them up. They turned out to be a pair of flesh-colored gloves. Katy put them on. They fitted perfectly. "Look, Louise," she said, "aren't these funny?"

"Aren't what funny?" Louise asked.

Katy stretched out her hands. "The gloves," she said.

"I don't see any gloves." Louise put down the bathrobe and pulled a pair of battered red rubber boots out of the drawer. "Your aunt never throws *any-thing* away, does she?"

Katy looked at the gloves again. They were the same color as her hands. She couldn't see them, and she couldn't even feel them.

Just then the doorbell rang.

"Mother must have forgotten to take her key. Quick, Louise, help me get the stuff back into the drawer." Katy put the rubber boots on top of a dented metal box that had a picture of a fruitcake on the lid.

Louise folded the bathrobe and stuffed it in with the other things. She put the little mirror on top and shut the drawer. Katy locked it and dropped the key into her pocket.

The doorbell rang again. Katy ran downstairs to answer it. A thin woman wearing a red raincoat and carrying a red umbrella stood on the doorstep. "Hello, Katy," she said.

"Oh, Miss Medwick!" said Katy. "Come

in. I forgot it was Tuesday." Tuesday
was the day for Katy's piano lesson.

The piano teacher came dripping into
the house. She closed her umbrella and
left it in the corner of the hall. Then she
took off her wet raincoat and gave it to
Katy to hang up.

Miss Medwick stood beside the piano bench and cracked her bony knuckles. "Come, Katy," she said, "let's see if you can do better this week. I hope you practiced your scales."

Katy hadn't been near the piano for days. There were always better things to do. She sat down on the bench and put her fingers on the keys. Suddenly she started to play. Her fingers ran through the scale without making a single mistake. When she finished she looked at Miss Medwick.

The piano teacher was smiling. "Katy!" she said. "That was just fine. Now let's hear *Swans on the Lake*." She opened the music book on the piano.

Katy played the little piece. She was surprised at how easy it was.

Miss Medwick looked at her in amazement. "Let's try something a bit harder, Katy," she said. She took a sheet of music out of the black folder that she always carried with her. She propped the music on the piano.

Katy stared at the jumble of nasty little black notes on the paper. The music looked much harder than anything she had ever played. "This is what I get for not making a mistake," she said to herself. "I won't do that again." Katy struck what she thought would be a sour note. No sooner had she touched the key when all the rest of her fingers began to move. She played the piece of music all the way through.

Louise had come downstairs and seated herself on the sofa at the other end of the living room. Katy looked at her. Louise didn't have her fingers in her ears the way she usually did when Katy played the piano. Today Louise sat and listened during the whole lesson.

When it was time for her to leave,

Miss Medwick seemed almost sorry to go. "You see what you can do when you really try, Katy," she said, as she put on her raincoat. "I'm so happy that all my work with you is finally showing results."

After Miss Medwick had gone, Louise said, "Katy, I didn't know you could play like that."

"It wasn't hard," Katy said. "I guess I never really tried before." She looked out of the window at the Brooklyn street. "It's stopped raining. Mother should be home soon. I'd better put these gloves away before she gets back."

Katy took off the gloves and ran upstairs to lock them away in the bottom drawer of the storage chest. Then she went back downstairs and sat down on the piano bench. She started to play *Swans on the Lake*. It wasn't as easy as before, but Katy played it to the end.

She looked up. Louise had her fingers in her ears.

"Is it really that bad?" Katy asked.

"You sound just the way you usually do."

Katy frowned. She bent over the piano keys and played the piece again.

There was the sound of a key in the lock of the front door. The door opened, and Mrs. Turner walked into the house.

"Hello, Mother," Katy said.

Mrs. Turner went to hang up her coat in the closet. "I heard you practicing the piano, Katy. How was your lesson?"

"Miss Medwick said it was much better than usual." Katy turned back to the music and played *Swans on the Lake* once more.

"That *is* better," said Mrs. Turner. "Don't you think so, Louise?"

Louise stood up. "I have to go now."

"I'll walk home with you," Katy said.

"Hurry back, Katy," said her mother. "It's almost suppertime."

Katy and Louise walked down the street under the dripping branches of the maple trees. The pavement was wet from the rain. Louise lived in a red brick apartment building around the corner from Katy's house.

Katy jumped over a puddle. "Playing the piano was different today," she said.

"It sure was," Louise told her. "I never heard you sound so good. No wonder your teacher was pleased. But then you went right back to playing the way you always do."

Katy was thinking so hard that she waded right through a puddle. "Louise," she said slowly, "do you suppose those funny gloves had anything to do with it?"

"Of course not," said Louise.

CHAPTER TWO

AFTER supper Katy played the piano again. Her father was reading the newspaper in the living room. "Katy," he said, "would you mind practicing some other time? I'm rather tired, and I could do with a little quiet."

Katy went upstairs. She knew it was silly but she kept thinking about the gloves. Before she started her homework she unlocked the bottom drawer of the storage chest. She found the gloves where she had tucked them in a corner. Katy put them on.

Her mother was coming down the hall. Katy shut the drawer so fast that her dress caught in it. When she stood up, Katy tore a small three-cornered rip near the hem of her dress.

Mrs. Turner opened the door and looked into the room. "How are you doing with your homework, Katy?"

"Fine," Katy said. She sat down at her desk and opened her spelling book. She wrote each word on her list five times. When she had finished she looked at the paper. Her handwriting seemed better than usual — much better. Katy went on to do the rest of her homework. Her arithmetic was finished in almost no time. Katy found herself making neat rows of numbers and adding and subtracting with no trouble at all.

When the homework was done, Katy remembered the tear in her dress. If she asked her mother to mend it, her mother would want to know how Katy had torn it. Katy decided to mend the dress herself.

She tiptoed down the hall to her mother's bedroom to get a needle and thread. Then she came back to her own room and took off her dress. She sat on the edge of her bed in her slip. The hardest part of sewing for Katy was threading the needle. She sucked the end of the thread and poked it at the eye of the needle. To her surprise it went right through.

Katy and Louise often sewed doll's clothes. Katy's stitches were always big and clumsy. Now she made tiny stitches and darned the torn edges together so that the lines of the plaid matched. It was hard to see that the dress had been torn.

Katy didn't even prick her finger. When she was done she looked at the dress. It didn't seem possible that she had done such a neat job. Then she remembered the gloves. She sat and thought for a long time.

"If they're magic," she said to herself, "there's one way to prove it."

Katy put on her dress and went downstairs to the piano. She played *Swans on the Lake.*

Mr. Turner was taking a nap behind his newspaper. When Katy finished playing he opened his eyes and said, "That's very pretty, Katy. Play it again."

CHAPTER THREE

NEXT morning Louise called for Katy after breakfast. They started to walk to school. Katy told Louise everything that had happened the night before.

"So you see," she finished, "the gloves *are* magic."

"All I know for sure," Louise said, "is that I never heard you play the piano like that before."

Katy opened her spelling notebook and handed it to Louise.

"Your handwriting certainly has improved," her friend said.

"That was the gloves," Katy told her. "If you don't believe me, try them yourself." She reached into her pocket and brought out the gloves.

Louise rubbed the thin stretchy cloth between her thumb and forefinger. "You know I'm left-handed, Katy. Why don't I wear the left glove and you wear the right one?"

Katy took back the right glove and slipped it on. Louise put on the left glove. Her hands were smaller than Katy's, but the glove fitted her perfectly too. Once the gloves were on their hands, they couldn't see or feel them.

Louise wanted to try her glove at once. She put her bookbag on the sidewalk, opened it, and took out a box of colored chalk. She squatted on her heels and began to draw a picture on the pavement.

Katy watched. Louise was always

drawing, but Katy had a feeling that this picture would be different.

Louise drew an Arab. He was dressed in long robes and held a curved sword. Behind him Louise put a desert and palm trees.

A lady who was hurrying along the street took a look at the picture. She stopped walking and stared at Louise. "Where did you learn to draw like that?" she asked.

"I never took any lessons," Louise said.

Two old men were leaning against an iron fence. They bent over to look at the picture on the pavement.

Louise added a few dark green marks to her palm trees.

By now there was a small crowd around the two girls. Louise was enjoying herself.

"You could make a fortune drawing like that," said one of the old men.

The lady looked at her watch. "I've got to go."

"What time is it?" Katy asked her.

"Five to nine," the lady said. She began to run toward the subway station.

Katy picked up Louise's bookbag and handed it to her. "Come on," she said. "We're fifteen minutes late already."

Louise put the chalk away in the bookbag and raced down the street after Katy.

The school yard was empty when they

got there. They had to go to the main office of the school and get late passes before they could go to their classroom.

Miss Johnson had already called the roll and marked them absent. Katy and Louise gave her their late passes. They went to their seats which were beside each other in the middle of the second row.

The teacher passed out papers for a spelling pre-test. Neither Louise nor Katy spelled any of the words wrong. That meant they wouldn't have spelling homework tonight.

Miss Johnson stood up. "Now, boys and girls," she said, "I want you all to put on your thinking caps. We're going to write an original story on *Good Citizenship*. Remember, these are to be your own ideas. It doesn't matter how long the story is. Just be sure it's the very best you can do."

Miss Johnson sat down at her desk and re-checked the spelling papers. The class set to work. Some of the children frowned and fiddled with their pens. Others started writing at once. Katy had no idea what to write. She put her name and the date at the top of the paper. After that she just kept writing until she had covered both sides of three pages. It was a little scary. Katy wasn't sure she could stop if she wanted to. Suddenly her pen made a period and her hand put the pen down.

"Time's up," Miss Johnson said. "Collect the papers, Michelle."

In the time left before lunch the children chose the actors for a play that the class was going to give for the rest of the school. It was a play about the first Thanksgiving Day. Miss Johnson had written it herself.

Katy was given the part of Priscilla

Mullins, the Pilgrim girl. It was the biggest part in the play. She would have to learn a lot of lines. Louise was chosen to play an Indian. She didn't have any lines at all.

When the bell rang for lunch the children filed out of the classroom. Some of them went down to the lunchroom in the basement of the school. Katy and Louise went home for lunch.

"Give me your glove, Louise," Katy said. "I'd better put both of them away before anything happens to them."

Louise took off the glove. "I wish I had one like it," she said. "Those people sure liked that picture I drew. It's funny, because I liked the princess I drew yesterday better."

CHAPTER FOUR

THE first thing Miss Johnson did in the afternoon was to change Katy's seat to one near the window. After that the children gave book reports. Then the class had a nature study lesson that lasted most of the afternoon. At three o'clock Miss Johnson said, "Will Katy Turner and Louise Adams please remain in their seats until the class has left."

After the other children had gone Miss Johnson said, "I moved you away from each other because it looks as if one of you has been copying. Not only are your spelling pre-tests just alike but so are your stories. You know I told you they were to be original." She handed Katy some papers. "Read those aloud," she said.

Katy read. She stumbled over some of the words. It was her own story — at least it had her name on it — but she couldn't remember any of it.

Miss Johnson gave her a sharp look. "It's a very good story, Katy," she said, "especially the part about not cheating."

"Katy didn't copy me, Miss Johnson," Louise said.

"It's nice of you to stand up for her, Louise," the teacher told her. "Now, let's hear *your* story."

Louise began to read very slowly. She couldn't remember the story either, but she'd just heard Katy read it. It was easier for her.

Miss Johnson nodded when Louise had finished. "Very nice, Louise," she said.

"Katy, I want you to go home and write *I must not copy other people's work* a hundred times. If you don't bring it to me tomorrow I'll have to send a note home to your parents. You may both go now."

The girls went quietly out of the school. They crossed the street and walked past a block of old frame houses. Katy began to skip along the walk.

"You don't seem to mind being punished," Louise said.

Katy stopped skipping and stooped to pet a striped orange kitten. "Oh, I guess I had it coming, Louise. Even if I wasn't copying I was still sort of cheating."

Louise stared at her.

Katy grinned. "How long do you suppose it would take to write a hundred lines — wearing the magic gloves?"

CHAPTER FIVE

KATY and Louise both failed the spelling re-test on Thursday. They had to do double homework because of it. When they were walking home from school Louise said, "I guess it's not a good idea to use the gloves in school, but they ought to be useful in other ways."

Katy played leapfrog over a fire hydrant. "I stopped using them when I practice the piano."

"Why?" Louise asked.

"Mother started talking about having Miss Medwick give me an hour lesson instead of a half hour. Daddy said it would cost a lot of money. Mother said they owed it to my talent. They almost had a fight about it. I took off the gloves and played *Swans on the Lake*. After that they both seemed happy to forget the whole thing."

Louise changed the subject. "We have to make costumes for the play. I'm going to sew beads on a blanket. I might as well have a nice costume. I don't have any lines to say."

"You could say, 'Ugh!' every so often," Katy suggested. "Miss Johnson couldn't stop you once you were up on the stage."

"She could give me a zero on my report card," Louise reminded her.

They had come to the brick archway in front of the apartment building where Louise lived. Louise said goodbye to Katy. "I'll come over to your house later." She went through the archway and into the building.

Katy hurried around the corner to her own house. Her mother answered the doorbell. Mrs. Turner had flour all over her hands and arms. She went back to the kitchen where she had been rolling out cookie dough.

Katy laid her books and her coat on a chair and opened the drawer where her mother kept her cookie cutters. "I have to have a costume for the school play, Mother. I've got the part of Priscilla Mullins." Katy handed her mother a cookie cutter that was shaped like a rabbit.

"Maybe we could fix up that old gray dress of mine," Mrs. Turner said. "I never wear it any more. There's a torn sheet in the linen closet that we could use to make a white collar and cuffs." She dipped the cookie cutter in flour and began to cut out rabbits.

"I might be able to make the costume

myself," Katy said. She knew her mother didn't like to sew.

"That would be wonderful." Mrs. Turner began to place the cookies on the cookie sheet. "Do you think you can sew well enough, Katy?"

"I can try," Katy said. "We learned a little sewing in school."

"If you run into trouble, I'll help you," her mother said. She put the cookie sheet into the oven. "Katy, go change out of your school clothes now."

A few minutes later Louise arrived. She was carrying a fluffy yellow blanket with a beautiful satin binding.

Her mother's old dress looked terribly plain to Katy now. Louise held up a glass tube filled with tiny colored beads. "I can sew these on a ribbon to make a headband."

The girls went upstairs, took the magic gloves out of the drawer, and put them on. Louise started to sew beads on her blanket. "Mother told me to take a blanket out of the cedar chest. This was down at the bottom, under some old army blankets."

"I think an army blanket would be better for an Indian," Katy said.

"Oh, you're just jealous." Louise sewed on a bright blue bead.

Katy and Louise couldn't spend much time on their sewing. They had a lot of spelling homework to do. "We can finish the costumes during the weekend," Louise said. The play was going to be performed for the whole school in the assembly on Monday morning.

On Friday afternoon Miss Johnson held a rehearsal on the stage in the auditorium. Louise knew Katy's lines better than Katy did. At one point Katy forgot what she had to say. There was a loud whisper from an Indian in the back of the stage. Miss Johnson glared at Louise.

All Saturday the girls sat on the floor in Katy's room and sewed. Katy decided to make a little white cap and an apron. The glove she was wearing had already made the changes in her mother's dress.

Mrs. Turner came upstairs to see how the costumes were coming along. She was astonished when she saw them. "They certainly did teach you sewing in school. I won't have to take up the hems of your skirts any more, Katy. You can do it yourself."

"Louise helped me," Katy said quickly. "She sews much better than I do."

"And you're left-handed too, Louise!" Mrs. Turner looked at the beautiful headband Louise was making.

When Katy's mother had gone back downstairs, Louise said, "Tell me about your Aunt Martha, Katy. Is she your mother's sister or your father's?"

Katy bit off her thread. "Neither. She's not a real aunt. She's a friend of Granny's. Mother always calls her Aunt Martha so I do too, even though I've never met her."

"Where is she now?" Louise put the last touches on a pattern of black and white beads.

Katy threaded a needle and started to sew a pocket on her apron. "I don't know. I sure hope she doesn't come back here and want the gloves before we finish the costumes."

"Mine's finished." Louise put down the headband and held up the blanket. It glittered with designs made of colored beads.

"Wow!" Katy said. "Mother promised to starch and iron my costume, but what's the use? Nobody's going to notice me when *you* walk onto the stage in that get-up."

CHAPTER SIX

K ATY didn't see Louise on Sunday. First thing Monday morning Louise rang her doorbell. She was carrying a brown paper package.

"Come in, Louise," Katy said. "I'll be ready to leave in a minute." She pulled her friend into the house. Now Katy saw that Louise's face was puffy, and her eyes were red as if she had been crying. "What's the matter, Louise?"

"Mother took away the yellow blanket." Louise's voice was husky. "She said she'd forgotten it was in the cedar chest. It's never been used. She said she couldn't let me drag it around a dirty stage. She cut the beads off and sewed them onto an army blanket."

"Let's see." Katy opened Louise's package. She looked at the blanket. Louise's mother had tried to do a good job, but her designs were not nearly as beautiful as those the magic gloves had sewn.

"We don't have time to fix this now," Katy said, "but I have an idea. Come upstairs." She ran up to her room and unlocked the bottom drawer of the storage chest. Katy pulled out the brightly-colored bathrobe. Then she grabbed some red and black jelly beans from the bag on her desk and put them into her pocket. She jammed the army blanket into the drawer and wrapped up the bathrobe in the brown paper.

"Do you have your headband?"

Louise nodded.

Katy went to the broom closet under the basement stairs and pulled two turkey feathers out of her mother's feather duster. She put on her coat and picked up the box in which her own costume was packed. "We've got to run, Louise. We'll be late again."

The two girls rushed out of the house and down the street. The first bell was ringing when they reached the schoolyard. They joined their line and marched into the school.

Miss Johnson didn't want the other classes in the school to see the costumes. She sent the children in her class backstage to put them on.

It was dark behind the stage. All the other children were busy with their own costumes. They didn't notice Katy and Louise. Katy took the jelly beans out of her pocket. She licked a black one and painted three stripes on each of Louise's cheeks. Louise stuck out her tongue to moisten a red jelly bean, and Katy drew a sunburst on her forehead. "Now you really look like an Indian."

Louise put on the headband, and Katy stuck the two turkey feathers in it. Then Katy took the gray dress out of her box while Louise unwrapped the bathrobe.

The gray dress reached all the way to the floor. Now that it was starched and ironed it looked very pretty. Katy tied the white apron around her waist and put on the little cap.

She had to be on the stage when the curtain went up. Katy tiptoed out and stood in front of a long table that was covered with cardboard cutouts of food. A group of children dressed as

Pilgrims was gathered around the table.

The curtain rose. Richard Higgins had the part of John Alden. He spoke first.

"We are having a feast to give thanks for a bountiful harvest."

Katy had the next line. She smoothed her apron and tried to remember it. Oh yes, "I'm glad we invited our Indian friends to share our good fortune. Here they come now."

Fifteen children dressed as Indians filed onto the stage. They were wrapped in blankets and shawls. Most of them had feathers in their hair. Two boys carried a deer made from cardboard, and one girl held a turkey of colored paper.

Louise was the last to come onto the stage. She had the smallest part of anybody in the play.

Katy wanted to see how the bathrobe

looked, but she couldn't see it at all. And she couldn't see the part of Louise that it covered. Instead Louise's head seemed to be floating in the air. Her face was bright with jelly bean warpaint, and the feathers in her headband stuck up proudly. The rest of Louise was invisible!

Katy stared. Suddenly she realized what had happened. The bathrobe was magic! If Louise had used the hood, her head would be invisible too.

The children on the stage were too busy with their parts to pay attention to Louise, but the children in the audience saw her. They began to howl with laughter. Everybody seemed to think this was some sort of trick, done with mirrors or luminous paint.

Miss Johnson saw Louise too. She was standing backstage in the wings. Katy could see her from where she stood. She thought Miss Johnson's face was turning a very funny color.

Katy had a great many lines to say. Now she could hardly remember them at all. At one point Richard Higgins looked at her and said, "Priscilla, let us now give thanks for all our blessings."

Katy couldn't think what she had to say. There was a long silence on the stage. Suddenly the floating head at the end of the row of Indians said in a loud whisper, "Katy, you're supposed to bow your head."

All the children on the stage turned to stare at Louise. One girl screamed, and the boys dropped the cardboard deer.

Louise didn't know her voice would sound so loud. She tried to hide behind one of the other Indians. The Indian dodged. He tripped over the cord to the microphone and knocked over the table. Panic spread across the stage. Pilgrims and Indians were running in circles. The

children in the audience were laughing
so hard that some of them were choking.

Katy moved over to Louise's floating
head. "Get off the stage," she whispered,
"and take off that bathrobe."

Louise was glad to get away from the
crowd. She didn't know what was wrong.
Everybody seemed to have gone crazy.

"Why do I have to take off the bathrobe, Katy? Is your mother in the audience? Do you think she'd recognize the bathrobe?"

"Look at yourself, Louise. Can you see yourself? Nobody else can." Katy pointed to where she thought Louise's feet should be.

Louise looked down. She poked her hands out of the long sleeves. They appeared in front of her. She kicked a foot out from under the robe. Louise untied the bathrobe and took it off. She folded it up. "Now, what can I use for a costume?"

"Don't worry about that now, Louise. Look at Miss Johnson!"

The teacher was lying on the floor near them. Her face was pale, and her eyes were closed.

Louise gasped, "Oh, Katy, is she dead?"

Katy kneeled down beside Miss Johnson. "She's breathing. I think she's fainted. Get some water, Louise." She began to rub Miss Johnson's hands.

Louise went out the stage door to the hall. She wet her handkerchief in the drinking fountain. When she came back she squeezed water out of the dripping handkerchief onto Miss Johnson's face.

The stage had been cleared by this time. The frightened children had been sent to take their places in the audience. Katy and Louise looked out at the stage. The principal was talking in front of the microphone.

"Boys and girls," he said, "I think we should all give Miss Johnson's class a big round of applause. I've seen a great many Thanksgiving plays in this school, but I never enjoyed any as much as this one. It was most unusual."

The children clapped wildly. Miss

Johnson opened her eyes and smiled at Katy and Louise. She was too weak to talk.

Katy carried both costumes home with her at lunchtime. She put the bathrobe away in the drawer and took out Louise's army blanket.

When she sat down to lunch, her mother asked, "How did the play go, Katy?"

"I forgot some of my lines, but it didn't matter," Katy told her.

"Well, you must do better next time," Mrs. Turner said.

During the afternoon the other children in the class kept asking Louise how she did her trick. Louise told them, "I'm practicing to be a magician, and I can't tell my secrets to anybody."

CHAPTER SEVEN

AFTER school Louise went home with Katy. She had to get the army blanket. "I'll play you a game of jacks before I go home."

"I can't find my jacks," Katy said. "I've been looking for them for ages."

"Forget the jacks then," Louise said. "I've been thinking. Your Aunt Martha has some mighty funny stuff in that drawer. I think we ought to try it all out. We might get into trouble if we don't know any more about it than we knew about the bathrobe."

Katy tried to look very proper. "We can't get into trouble if we don't touch the stuff."

Louise stared at her.

Katy grinned. "But since we're sure to touch it, we'd better check it over first."

The girls went upstairs to Katy's bedroom. Katy shut the door and pushed her bed against it. "If Mother starts to come in, this will give us time to put the things back in the drawer."

Louise put her school books on the bed and went over to the chest of drawers in the corner of the room. "Where's the key, Katy?"

Katy took the worn old key out of her pocket and handed it to her. Louise opened the bottom drawer of the chest. "Katy, you've got these things all mixed up. The mirror is supposed to be on top."

"You're such a fusspot, Louise." Katy took out the bathrobe and found the mirror under it. "Here, is this what you're looking for?"

Louise held the mirror by its dainty carved handle. She looked into the glass. "Funny," she said. "It's cloudy. I can't see a thing."

"Give it to me," Katy said. "Mirror, mirror, on the wall, who is the fairest one of all?"

Louise answered in a deep, singsong voice. "You are, Katy. Can't you see? Why else would Priscilla Mullins you be?"

"Oh, Louise, can't you forget that?" Katy put down the mirror. "You know nobody even *saw* Priscilla Mullins when that Indian head was bobbing around on the stage."

Louise picked up the mirror again. She stared into it. "I can't see my face in it. I don't know what it's good for, but it certainly isn't an ordinary mirror."

"What else is in the drawer?" Katy asked.

Louise laid the little mirror on the floor. "Just these old boots and the tin box." Louise picked up the red rubber boots and turned them over. "Look, Katy, something is stamped on the sole."

Katy read, "*Made in Germany*. There's something else, Louise. It's written very small."

Louise looked hard at the tiny letters. "*Seven League Boots*. Weren't they in an old story, Katy?"

"Of course," Katy said. "It was *Hop o' My Thumb*. Don't you remember? You could go very fast with them. Each step was seven leagues long."

"What's a league?" Louise asked.

Katy went downstairs to get the big

dictionary from the living room book-
case. She came back and pushed the
bed back against the door.

Katy sat down on the floor beside
Louise and opened the book. "*Lead,
leaf,* here it is: *league* — about three
miles." Katy chewed the end of a piece
of her hair. "Seven leagues, that's more
than twenty miles."

"Twenty-one," Louise said. "We'll
have to be careful with those boots.
I'm not sure I want to take a step and
be twenty-one miles away and all by
myself. We can't both use them at the
same time."

"Why not?" Katy asked. "We could
each put on one boot and then hop."

Louise thought about it. "It's worth
a try. If we held hands we could stay
together."

Katy put the dictionary on the floor.
Louise picked up the dented metal box

with the picture of a fruitcake on the lid. Inside it she found a set of six jacks and a little red rubber ball.

"Those are the jacks I've been looking for," Katy said. "I wonder how they got in there."

At that moment Katy heard her mother coming up the stairs. She shoved the mirror, the bathrobe, and the boots back into the drawer. Louise dropped the metal box, and the jacks scattered across the floor. The ball rolled under the bed. Katy put the empty box back in the drawer and closed it. She jumped to her feet and moved the bed away from the door.

Mrs. Turner opened the door and looked into the room. "You haven't changed out of your school clothes yet, Katy. I thought you and Louise would like to come downstairs and pop some corn."

"We'll be down in a minute," Katy said. She slipped off her skirt. Louise started to gather the jacks. The ball was stuck between the bed and the wall. Katy had to crawl on her stomach to get it. She gave it to Louise and began to put on a pair of blue jeans.

Mrs. Turner had gone back downstairs.

"What do you want me to do with the jacks?" Louise asked.

"Let's play with them after we've popped the corn," Katy said.

"I could only find five of them," Louise told her.

Katy pulled on a polo shirt. She got down on all fours to help Louise look for the other jack. They searched all over the room, but they didn't find it.

"We might as well put the jacks back in the box," Katy said at last. "We can't play with just five." She pulled out the drawer and picked up the metal box. When she opened it she found the sixth jack inside. "I was sure the box was empty when I put it away," Katy said. "Well, anyway, we've got all the jacks now." She dropped them into her pocket and put the box back in the drawer.

The two girls went downstairs to pop the corn.

CHAPTER EIGHT

On Tuesday afternoon, Louise again went to Katy's house after school. Katy was waiting for Miss Medwick to come and give her a piano lesson.

"When are we going to try out the boots, Katy?" Louise asked.

"Why not Friday?" Katy sat down at the piano bench. "Thursday is Thanksgiving, and Friday is a holiday too." She began to play a scale.

Louise put her fingers in her ears. "I wish you would use the magic gloves," she said. "Where shall we go with the boots?"

"Florida," Katy said. "We can go swimming."

The doorbell rang. It was Miss Medwick.

"Goodbye, Katy. I'll see you tomorrow." Louise ran out of the house before Katy could start her music lesson.

When they were walking home after school on Wednesday, Katy told Louise, "Ask your mother if you can go on a picnic Friday."

Louise looked at the bare trees. "I don't think she'll let me at this time of year."

"Well, ask her if you can eat lunch at my house then," Katy said. "That should give us time to try out the boots."

Louise walked along in silence. She was thinking. "Katy," she said, "we shouldn't go anywhere without a map. Stop at my house before you go home."

When they reached the brick archway, Katy and Louise went through it and into the building where Louise lived. They took the elevator to the fifth floor. Louise rang the doorbell of apartment 5H. Her mother opened the door. Mrs. Adams was holding a pen and a paper. She had been writing a letter. "Hello, Katy," she said. "How was school, Louise?"

"Fine," Louise said. "Mom, do we have a map of the United States?"

"There's one in the Atlas," Mrs. Adams said, "but I think we have a newer one. It's in last month's *Geographic*." She picked up a thick yellow magazine from the marble-topped coffee table. A map was folded into it. Mrs. Adams pulled it out and gave it to Louise. "This ought to help you," she said. She went to the kitchen to finish writing her letter there.

Katy and Louise spread the map out

on the rug.

"Why do we need a map of the whole country?" Katy asked. "We only want to go to Florida."

Louise wasn't listening. She got down on her hands and knees on the soft rug to study the map. "Five steps would take us over a hundred miles."

"Five hops, you mean." Katy started hopping around the room to practice.

"Stop it, Katy!" said Louise. "My mother is always afraid we might break something in the living room. Come and look at the map. We have to decide where we're going."

Katy took one more hop. "South," she said. "Bring your bathing suit."

Friday morning was gray and wet. Katy was sure her mother wouldn't let her go on a picnic. She went to the kitchen after breakfast and peeked into the refrigerator. It was full of leftovers from yesterday's turkey dinner.

When Mrs. Turner went to the basement with a load of laundry, Katy dropped the turkey's neck and wings into a brown paper bag with four apples. Then she took all but three of the cookies in the jar on the kitchen table. As an afterthought she added a handful of walnuts and two cans of ginger ale.

Mrs. Turner was coming up the basement stairs. Katy ran out of the kitchen and took the sack of food to her room.

Two minutes later Louise rang the doorbell. Katy came down to let her in. Louise was wearing a raincoat and boots and carrying an umbrella. "Look what I found in my father's desk." She held out a compass. It was a real compass, not just a toy. The case was made of shining brass, and the needle had a pretty shape.

Katy held the compass and admired it

while Louise took off her boots. She left them with her umbrella just inside the front door. "Mother doesn't expect me home till dinner time."

Katy looked at Louise's boots. "They look just like the ones in the drawer," she said.

Louise nodded. "Only these are made in Finland."

Mrs. Turner came out of the kitchen. "Good morning, Louise," she said. "It's such a nasty day. Why don't you stay for lunch? We have a lot of leftovers to eat up."

"Mother," Katy said, "Louise and I promised to help a friend with her homework. She wants us to stay for lunch."

Mrs. Turner took the vacuum cleaner out of the hall closet. "What's your friend's name, Katy? Does she live near here? Don't you think you should give me her telephone number? Are you sure her mother expects you for lunch?"

Katy took a deep breath and decided to answer the third question. "I don't know her phone number, Mother. I'll be home early. Come on, Louise." She ran upstairs before her mother could say anything else.

Louise followed Katy up to her room.

"Did you remember your bathing suit?" Katy whispered.

"I couldn't find it," Louise said. "My mother has all my summer things packed away."

Katy unlocked the bottom drawer of the chest and pulled out the boots.

"What a mess this drawer is, Katy! I thought we were going to keep everything in the right place." Louise kneeled down and started to straighten the things in the drawer.

"Hurry up," Katy said. "We'd better leave before my mother changes her mind about letting me go." She grabbed the paper bag of food from under her bed.

Louise closed the drawer and locked it. She gave Katy the key. Katy put on her raincoat and rain hat. She took the right boot and handed the left one to Louise. "Wait till we're outside before you put it on. I don't want you making holes in the walls of the house."

In the front hall Louise put on one of her own boots and gave the other to Katy. She picked up the umbrella.

It was cold outdoors, and it was still raining. The girls sat under the umbrella on the wet front steps of Katy's house to put on the boots. When they stood up Louise took out the beautiful compass. Both of them studied it for a minute.

"We'd better keep our feet together," Katy said. "We're carrying too much to hold hands. Give me the compass, Louise.

You take charge of the umbrella. Now, hop!"

"Wait a minute!" Louise said. "Why do we have to hop? I've a better idea. If we just walk, one foot will take us twenty-one miles. The other will only go one step. We won't get tired that way. I've never been very good at hopping."

"We have to be careful," Katy said. "It would be awful if you took a step with the ordinary boot when I took one with the magic boot."

Louise placed her left foot tight against Katy's right. "Which way are we facing?" she asked.

"Southwest," Katy said. "Ready?"

"Ready!" Louise answered.

As if they were glued together, the girls stepped forward.

CHAPTER NINE

KATY and Louise were standing at the corner of a street they had never seen before. The houses looked newer than the ones in Brooklyn, and they all had big yards. Ahead of them a traffic light glowed red. A stream of cars whizzed by.

"We're lucky we didn't land in the middle of the street," Louise said.

Katy looked at the compass and then at the traffic signal. "The light's green now. Step with your other foot."

They took one step into the street with the feet that wore Louise's boots. "Now!" said Katy. Again they stepped with the magic boots. This time they found themselves in a field of wet brown grass.

They walked a step in the field and then stepped all the way to the edge of

a highway. It wasn't raining now. Louise closed the umbrella.

They went from the highway to a city street, to the bank of a river, to a forest with leaves rustling on the ground.

Katy sniffed the air. It smelled of pine. "I wonder where we are."

"We should have counted our steps," Louise said. "Oh well, the main thing is to walk in the right direction."

They studied the compass. "Step toward that tree," said Katy, "the big one with the double trunk."

They took a step which brought them close to the pine tree and then one which landed them on a wide green lawn in front of a large house.

"Look!" Louise screamed.

A huge dog was racing toward them. His teeth were bared, and there was a fierce look in his eyes.

"Don't look. Walk!" Katy gasped.

Two steps and the dog had disappeared. They were on a highway again. The sky above them was blue. For a while they walked along the highway. The wide straight road seemed to stay the same for several steps. Only the view changed.

The weather was getting warmer. Louise took off her raincoat and unzipped the woolly lining. She put the coat back on and carried the lining. Katy took off her wet rain hat and stuffed it into her pocket. Then she took off her coat. She was wearing a sweater under it.

"As soon as we find a good place for our picnic, we'll take off the boots," Katy said.

A few steps more brought them to a garden. Yellow roses bloomed on a bush beside them. Katy bent down to pull off her boots.

Louise yanked her upright again.

"Katy Turner, this is probably the back-yard of another big house with a dog."

"You're right," they heard a deep voice say. "What are you doing here?"

A man wearing overalls stood in front of them. He was holding a rake and frowning.

Both girls had the same idea. They took two steps toward the man. By the time they finished the second step they couldn't see him any more.

"Do you suppose we walked *through* him?" Katy asked.

"I didn't feel it if we did." Louise looked around. Now they were standing on a hilltop. Rolling wooded hills were all around them. "This looks like a great place for a picnic," Louise said.

Katy looked at the hills in the distance. "I wonder if we can just step from hill to hill. Let's try."

It was a lovely idea. Together the girls

began to walk across the range of hills. Suddenly the hills were gone. A few steps more and they were on a flat plain.

"Let's go back, Katy," Louise said. "I liked the hills better."

"Oh, we'll come to some more hills," Katy said.

She was right. They did come to more hills. They were brown and stony with no big trees on them. The bushes on them looked more gray than green. Katy and Louise walked faster. Soon the ground was flat again. Spiky thick plants grew out of it. The sun was so warm that Louise took off her raincoat and Katy tied her sweater around her waist.

"I'm hungry," Louise said. "Let's stop here."

"There's no shade, and it's hot," Katy argued. "Just a few more steps, Louise. I'd like a tree to sit under."

"Oh, all right." Louise put the lining

back in her raincoat and looped the coat over her arm. "Ready?"

They walked a little farther. The ground wasn't flat any more. Far off they could see a line of mountains. The mountains looked bare, but the land around them was covered with flowers, and there were clumps of bushes at the roadside.

Over to the right they could see a group of white houses. It seemed to be a little town or village.

"Where do you suppose we are now?" Katy asked.

"I don't care. I'm hungry." Louise sat down at the edge of the road and pulled off her boots.

Katy put down her raincoat and the paper bag. She bent down and took off her boots too.

CHAPTER TEN

Someone was coming around the bend of the gravel road. Katy and Louise were surprised to see a girl riding on a fuzzy gray donkey. Her hair was in two shiny braids tied with red ribbons, and she wore a pretty blouse embroidered with blue flowers. The girl rode up to them and stopped. *"Buenos días,"* she said with a friendly smile.

Miss Johnson had been trying to teach Spanish to her class. Katy and Louise hadn't learned much, but they did know what *Buenos días* meant.

"Good day to you," Katy said.

"Hello," said Louise.

"You are American!" the girl said. "I learn English in school."

"Yes," Katy said. "Louise," she said in a low voice, "we must be in Mexico!"

"I am happy to meet you," the girl said. "My name is Pilar." She climbed down from her donkey and held out her hand.

Katy shook Pilar's hand. "I'm Katy," she said. "This is Louise."

Pilar shook hands with Louise too. She pointed to the donkey. "This is Pepe."

"Hello, Peppy," Katy patted the donkey's furry neck.

"You like to ride him?" Pilar asked.

"Oh, yes," Katy said.

Louise wasn't sure. "Does he bite?" she wanted to know.

"Bite?" Pilar didn't seem to understand.

Katy showed her teeth and snapped at Louise. "Bite," she explained.

Pilar laughed. "No bite," she said.

"Why don't we eat first and ride the donkey afterward?" said Louise. "Maybe Pilar will share our picnic."

Again Pilar didn't understand. Louise spoke too fast for her. Pilar looked at Katy for help.

Katy pointed to Louise and to herself. "We eat," she said, and pointed into her mouth. She opened the paper bag to show Pilar the food inside. "You eat too, Pilar."

Pilar shook her head.

"Please, Pilar," said Katy. She pulled a broken chocolate chip cookie out of the bag and gave it to the Mexican girl.

"*Gracias*," Pilar said. She looked at the cookie and took a small polite bite. "Good," she said. She seemed surprised that she liked the cookie.

"Of course it's good." Katy spread her raincoat like a tablecloth on the rough grass at the roadside. Then she took the pieces of turkey, the apples, nuts, cookies, and cans of ginger ale out of the paper bag and set them on the raincoat.

Pilar looked at the food spread out before her. The cookies were crumbled, but everything else was in good shape. Katy set up the umbrella over the feast as a final touch.

Louise pulled the top off a can. It popped and fizzed. She took a sip of the ginger ale and handed the can to Pilar.

Pilar swallowed a mouthful. The bubbles went up her nose. She coughed and sneezed. Katy banged her on the back and gave her a turkey wing to chew on.

All three girls settled down to eat. Pilar found a flat stone. They put the walnuts on it and banged them with another stone to crack them open.

When the last cookie was finished, Pilar said, "Give me the empty cans. My friend Antonio makes things out of them."

Katy gave her the cans. "Now we have to ride Peppy," she said.

The donkey was standing in the shade of a scrubby little tree. He nibbled the grass at the edge of the road.

"What's in there?" Louise pointed to the two big baskets the donkey carried, one on each side of him.

Pilar went over to the donkey and pulled an armful of damp straw out of one of the baskets. She looked at it for a minute.

Katy could see that something was wrong. Pilar looked as if she were going to cry. "What's the matter, Pilar?" she asked.

"It's late," Pilar said. "I forgot. I must work." She sat down and began to braid the straw. She worked as fast as she could. "Grandmother needs them for the market tomorrow."

"What's she making, Katy?" Louise asked.

"I don't know. If only we'd had the sense to bring the magic gloves we could help her," Katy said.

Louise walked over to where her raincoat was neatly folded on the grass. She pulled something out of a pocket. "One of us *did* have the sense." Louise handed a glove to Katy.

Katy and Louise sat one on each side of Pilar and watched her. Soon they saw that she was making a place mat for a table setting.

Katy put the magic glove on her right hand and picked up a long strand of straw. She began to twist it in and out of other strands as she saw Pilar doing. In a very short time she had finished a pretty mat, even though she did all the work with her right hand. She used her left just to hold things steady.

Louise was slower. She was making fancy designs in her mat.

Pilar was so busy working that she didn't notice what Louise and Katy were doing. It was only when she found that her pile of straw was all gone that she looked up. She saw two stacks of finished place mats on Katy's spread out raincoat.

"Good?" Katy asked.

"Good!" Pilar said. She looked at Louise's fancy mats. "Very good."

Pilar took another armful of straw out of the other basket. The three girls worked in silence until it too was all gone.

"Now," said Katy, "let's ride Peppy."

Pilar helped her to climb on the donkey's back and showed her how to guide him. Katy bounced down the dirt road.

She patted the donkey's flanks to make him go faster, but Pepe stopped suddenly and wouldn't go at all.

Pilar ran down the road after Pepe and talked to him in Spanish. He turned around and trotted back to where Louise was waiting.

When Katy got off the donkey's back she pulled off her glove and gave it to Louise. "Better keep them both together," she said.

Louise climbed up on the donkey and put her arms around his furry neck. She hung on as Pepe galloped down the road at top speed.

Katy and Pilar chased after him. They were out of breath by the time the donkey stopped.

Louise grabbed Pilar's hand and jumped down to the road. "Thank you, Pilar," she said. "I'd rather walk. Katy, didn't you promise your mother you'd be home early?"

Katy looked at the sun. It was getting low in the sky. "We have to go home now, Pilar," she said.

Pilar nodded. "I go home too."

Katy and Louise helped Pilar load the place mats into Pepe's baskets. Pilar waved her hand and led the donkey away down the road toward the little white town.

Louise was careful to see that they didn't mix up the boots. She checked the labels and handed Katy the right German boot and the left Finnish boot. Then she sat down beside her on a grassy bank and put the others on her own feet. They picked up the raincoats and the umbrella and stood up.

Katy took out the beautiful compass. Together the girls turned to face northeast, and together they took a step with the seven league boots.

It was dark and cold when Katy and Louise came home. They had been walking away from the sun.

Katy sat down on the front steps of her house and pulled off both her boots. She gave Louise her own boot and took back the magic one. Then Louise opened the umbrella and marched off in the rain toward home.

"You're late, Katy," Mrs. Turner said when Katy came into the house. "I hope you were able to help your friend with her work. Next time you must give me her telephone number."

CHAPTER ELEVEN

Right after breakfast on Saturday morning Louise rang Katy's doorbell.

Katy opened the door. "What did you do with the magic gloves, Louise?"

"I don't remember," Louise said. "Don't you have them?"

"No," Katy told her. "I took mine off when my donkey ride was over. I thought I gave it to you."

"If you did I must have put it in my raincoat pocket with the other one," Louise said. "Come on over to my house, and we'll get them."

They went to Louise's apartment to look for the gloves. They were not in her raincoat pocket.

"Maybe you dropped them on the road when Peppy started to gallop," Katy said. "Let's go back and look for them. If we hurry it won't take us long to get them."

The girls took Louise's father's compass and went back to Katy's house. Katy closed the door to her room and unlocked the bottom drawer of the chest in the corner.

"I wish I could see Pilar's grandmother selling those mats we made," Louise said. She looked over Katy's shoulder and caught sight of the little silver mirror in the drawer.

Louise took it out and gazed into it. "Katy, look!"

The mirror was like a tiny color television set. It made no sound, and yet the picture in it looked more alive than any they had ever seen.

Katy put her head close to Louise's so

that they could both look into the mirror. What they saw was a market. Squares of white canvas were stretched above the stalls to keep off the bright sunlight. People were selling pottery, dried beans and fish, huge bunches of flowers, guitars, and all sorts of other things.

An old woman sat on the ground, surrounded by baskets. A man was talking to her. Katy and Louise saw him pick up something from a pile in front of the woman.

"It's one of your mats, Louise!" Katy said.

The man leaned over and shuffled through the pile of mats. He sorted out all the fancy ones that Louise had made. Then he said something to the woman, and she nodded.

Katy put the mirror away. "OK Louise, we've found out what the mirror is good for," she said, "but we don't have time to play with it now. We have to go after the gloves."

"I still don't understand," Louise said. "Why would the mirror show us *that*?"

"It's a wishing mirror," Katy explained. "You wished to see Pilar's grandmother selling the mats. Now, hurry up. We've got to get back to Mexico."

The girls locked the drawer and tip-toed downstairs with the boots. It wasn't raining today, but the air was sharp and cold. They both wore sweaters with jackets over them. This way they could take off one thing at a time as they went south.

Katy and Louise strode along, each wearing one boot. They whizzed right past the big dog. The angry man in overalls was clipping a hedge. He glanced up when they stepped into his garden. Louise thought he looked rather sick when he saw them, but they didn't stop to ask about his health. Two steps and they were far away.

In less time than it would take to walk around the block they were back on the dusty road in Mexico.

The sunlight was glaring today. They had tied their sweaters around their waists. Their jackets were over their arms. Now they took off the boots, and Katy carried them.

Louise searched in the grassy bank where they had worked on the mats. Katy walked zig-zag along the road where the donkey had galloped. They looked in the bushes at the roadside. There was no sign of the gloves anywhere.

"Maybe someone found them and picked them up," Katy said at last. "If we could find Pilar, she might know."

They started walking along the road toward the little town. When they

reached it they found a market set up in the square in the center of the town. "This is what we saw in the mirror," Katy said. "That looks like the place where Pilar's grandmother was selling the mats."

"But there's no one here," Louise said. She walked over to the empty stall. The piles of baskets were gone.

"We're too late," said Katy.

At that moment she felt a tap on her shoulder. She turned to see Pilar. Katy was so happy to see her that she hugged her.

Pilar looked happy too. She hugged both Katy and Louise.

"Pilar," Katy said, "did you find the gloves?"

Pilar crinkled her eyebrows. She didn't seem to understand.

Katy held out her hands and pretended to be putting on gloves. "Gloves,

gloves," she said, "we lost gloves."

Pilar shook her head. She turned to Louise. "Grandmother sold all the pretty mats. She wants more. Show me how you make them, *por favor*, Louise."

Katy said, "That means *please*, Louise. Now what do we do?"

"I don't know," said Louise. "I can't show Pilar how to make the mats. I don't know how I did it. It was the magic gloves."

Just then Louise stopped talking and gave a little scream. The donkey had come up behind her and put his cold nose on her neck.

Pilar laughed. "I think Pepe likes you." Then she frowned. "He is bad burro. I look everywhere for him since yesterday."

Katy was staring at the donkey. "Louise!" she said in a low voice. "What are those things on his ears?"

Pepe looked very strange. He seemed to have a little stocking cap on each ear, and he did not look happy. Louise thought he wanted her to take them off. He kept twitching his ears.

Louise was afraid of the donkey's big teeth, but he looked at her with such sad brown eyes that she had to help him. She pulled off first one little cap and then the other.

As soon as she felt them Louise knew what they were, but she had to look to be sure. "Katy," she whispered, "they're the magic gloves. They must have flipped onto Peppy's ears when I was riding him yesterday."

Pilar put her arms around the donkey's neck. "Poor Pepe," she said. "He hates things on his ears. Now I know why he ran away."

The shaggy little donkey looked happy now. He kicked up his heels and galloped across the square. The three girls chased after him.

CHAPTER TWELVE

Pᴵᴸᴬᴿ caught up with the donkey in front of a stall where a boy was selling pottery. She grabbed hold of the rope that dangled from the donkey's neck.

"Look, Katy." Louise pointed to a set of tiny clay dishes in the stall. "They're just the right size for my doll's house. Daddy gave me my allowance this morning." She turned to Pilar. "Can I buy things with American money here?"

Pilar put her finger to her lips. "I will help you," she said. "What do you want to buy?"

Louise showed her the dishes. They were glazed green and brown and had a little tray to go with them.

Pilar started talking to the boy who was selling the pottery. The two of them spoke in Spanish and so fast that neither Katy nor Louise could understand a single word. Pilar seemed to be arguing with the boy. At last she shook her head and walked away from the stall.

Louise was disappointed. She wanted the dishes.

"Come," said Pilar.

Louise wanted to go back to the stall, but Pilar pulled her by the hand. Before they had gone very far the boy ran after them. He held the little tray of dishes and called something to Pilar.

"He wants five cents," Pilar said.

Louise couldn't believe her ears. She thought the dishes would cost much more. She gave the boy a nickel and took the set of dishes.

Pilar was grinning. When the boy had gone back to his stall, she said, "He asked for too much money. When he saw you would not give it to him, he sold the dishes at the right price."

The girls walked all around the market place. They stopped to look at the big bunches of lilies and carnations. Pilar took them to a stall where an old man was selling tin masks and lanterns. "This is Antonio," Pilar said. "He makes these things from tin cans." Katy and Louise shook hands with Antonio.

In one corner of the market a young man was selling what looked like ordinary walnuts that had been varnished. Katy looked closer and saw that the walnuts had little doors in them that shut with tiny hinges. One shell had four little doors cut into it. They swung open to show a bride and groom standing under an arch. The doors folded down like platforms and on each stood a wedding guest, holding out his arms. The little figures were made of wire and cloth and sprinkled with gold and silver glitter. Katy looked at the walnut wedding for a long time.

"Do you want it, Katy?" Pilar asked.

"I only have a dime." Katy took the coin out of her pocket and showed it to Pilar.

"I'll try to buy it for you, Katy." Pilar went over to the young man and talked to him for a long time in a low voice. At last the man nodded. "Give him the money, Katy," Pilar said.

Katy handed her dime to the young man, and he gave her the walnut shell. Katy opened it and looked at the dainty figures inside. She had never seen anything like it. The young man watched her and smiled.

"He says he sold it to you because you want it so much," Pilar told her.

The Mexican girl had let go of the donkey's rope. Suddenly he started to trot. He turned out of the market square into one of the narrow side streets of the town. Pilar ran after him, and Katy and Louise followed her.

Pepe stopped in front of a low white house. Pilar opened the door. "Come in," she said.

Pilar led the donkey inside. Katy and Louise followed her down a long hall and through an arched doorway into a sunny courtyard. Pilar put Pepe into a stable on one side of it.

The courtyard was completely hidden from the street. It seemed like a secret garden. There was a well in the middle.

All around were flowering plants in large stone pots.

An old woman sat in the shade of an overhanging roof of red clay tiles. She was dressed in black and was busy weaving a basket. Pilar ran up to her and said something in Spanish. The old woman looked up at Katy and Louise and smiled. She held out her hand to them. Katy and Louise shook hands with her, and then the old woman went back to working on her basket.

Pilar reached into a big jar and brought out a handful of wet straw. "Show me how you make your mats, Louise," she said.

Louise put on both the magic gloves.

"I'm afraid they'll work too fast," she whispered to Katy.

"Try asking them to go slow," Katy suggested.

Pilar went to a different jar and brought back some green and some red straw.

There was a small tree growing on one side of the courtyard. Yellow lemons peeked out from between the shiny dark green leaves on its branches. Louise sat on a stone bench under the tree. She was glad to get out of the heat of the sun. She spread her jacket on her lap and picked up two pieces of damp straw. Then she set to work. Pilar sat on one side of her and Katy on the other. Louise worked as slowly as she could. She began to braid the straw together.

Pilar watched every move Louise's fingers made. "*Si, si,*" she said.

When Louise had finished making the

mat, Pilar took some straw and began to braid. She started to make a mat just like the one Louise had finished. Katy wondered how she did it. She had been watching Louise too, but she couldn't even remember how to begin.

At one point Pilar stopped and looked at Louise. "I forget what to do now," she said.

Louise picked up Pilar's mat with the magic gloves. "Watch," she said to the Mexican girl. To the gloves she silently said, "Slow, slow, *slow*!"

Her hands in the gloves put two pieces of colored straw together and twisted them in and out of the half-finished mat.

"Now I see." Pilar took back the mat and began to work again. This time she didn't stop until she finished the mat. Then she ran over to her grandmother to show her what she had done. The old woman held up the mat and nodded.

"*Bella!*" she said.

Katy jumped up from the bench. "Louise," she said, "it's getting late." She went over to Pilar and her grandmother. "Goodbye. We have to go home now."

Pilar's grandmother picked up two little baskets. She gave one to Katy and one to Louise.

"Grandmother wants to give you a present," Pilar said.

"Thank you." Katy grabbed Louise's hand. Together they walked down the hall and out into the street. Katy put her walnut and the magic gloves into her basket, and Louise put the set of little dishes into hers. Katy handed Louise the left boot. She shoved her own foot into the right one. Louise held the compass. They put their feet together and took a step to the northeast.

CHAPTER THIRTEEN

I T was long past lunchtime when Katy came home. Her mother was very angry. "Where were you, Katy?"

"I was with Louise," Katy told her.

"I telephoned Louise's mother. You weren't at her house."

"We were shopping," Katy said. "Louise got her allowance this morning." Katy held the seven league boots behind her back with the little basket.

Her mother looked to see what she was hiding. "What are you doing with Louise's boots?"

"I was carrying them for her," Katy said.

"Well, put them in your room and remind Louise to take them home. Then come into the kitchen and get something to eat."

Katy ran upstairs to her room. She threw her jacket and her sweater on the bed and crammed the boots and gloves into the drawer. She locked the drawer and dropped the key into her pocket. Then she put the basket with the walnut in it on top of her desk and went back downstairs to eat her lunch.

The doorbell rang just as Katy was finishing her milk. Louise was at the door. "Katy," she said, "I've got trouble."

Katy took her upstairs to her room. "What's the matter, Louise?"

"My father is looking for his compass, and *I can't find it*," Louise said.

"We were in an awful hurry when we left Mexico," Katy said. "Do you think you dropped the compass then?"

"Katy, what shall I do?" Louise said. "My father's awfully mad."

"Maybe it fell into the boot." Katy unlocked the drawer and took out the things in it one by one. She turned each boot upside down and shook it. Louise unfolded the bathrobe to see if the compass might be caught in the cloth. Katy squeezed the gloves to make sure that nothing was hidden in them.

Louise took a look in the little mirror. She put it down fast.

"What's the matter?" Katy asked her. "What did you see in it, Louise?"

"My father," Louise said. "He was glaring at me. Why would I see *him*?"

"You must have been thinking about him," Katy decided.

"I can't think of anything else," Louise said.

Katy had an idea. She picked up the mirror and said, "I wish I knew where the compass is." The mirror darkened and changed.

Katy and Louise stared into the glass. They couldn't be sure what it was they saw. "I think I see the compass," Katy said. "But it's dark all around. I can't tell where it is."

"I guess there's no way of finding it," Louise said. "I wonder how much a compass like that costs. Maybe I could buy a new one for my father. I have the money I was saving to buy a bicycle pump."

Katy put down the mirror and picked up the metal box with the picture of the fruitcake on the lid. Something inside it rattled. "I thought this box was empty," Katy said. She opened it. The missing compass was inside.

Both girls stared at it. "I know *I* didn't put it there," Louise said. "Katy, are you playing a joke on me?"

Katy shook her head. "I don't know how it got there any more than you do."

"Well, I don't care how it got there. I'm just glad to get it back." Louise took the compass out of the box. "I've got to put it where my father will find it. See you later, Katy." She ran out of the room and down the stairs. Katy heard the front door bang as Louise went out.

Katy folded the bathrobe and put it back into the drawer. She could hear her mother coming up the stairs. Quickly she scooped up the boots and the gloves from the floor and dropped them on top of the bathrobe. She had just time to put in the little mirror and close the drawer when her mother opened the door of her room. Katy noticed that she had forgotten to put away the metal box with the picture of the fruitcake on it. She gave it a shove with her foot and pushed it under the bed.

Mrs. Turner was carrying a pile of clean laundry. She put three pairs of

Katy's socks in her dresser. "That's a pretty basket, Katy," she said. "Where did you get it?"

"The grandmother of the girl Louise and I helped with her work gave it to me. She made it herself."

"I've heard they teach basket weaving at the Golden Age Center." Mrs. Turner put away a pile of underwear in Katy's dresser. "Where's Louise?"

"She had to go home," Katy said. "I think she's coming back."

The doorbell rang. Katy went downstairs to answer it.

Louise was standing on the front stoop with a big grin on her face. "I put the compass on my father's desk underneath the big paperweight that looks like a giant frog. When he found it, Daddy said he didn't know why he hadn't looked there before. He locked it away in his desk."

CHAPTER FOURTEEN

K<small>ATY</small> was in the kitchen watching her mother clean the stove. "Tell me about Aunt Martha."

Mrs. Turner looked surprised. "I didn't think you'd ever met her, Katy, but she sent you a present when you were a baby."

"I never did meet her," Katy said. "What was the present?"

"A rattle," her mother told her. "Daddy and I used to call it 'the magic rattle' because you stopped crying any time we gave it to you. I don't know what happened to it. Somehow it was lost."

She opened the oven door and took out the racks.

"But what is Aunt Martha like?" Katy persisted.

"I don't know her very well," Mrs. Turner said. "She was a friend of Granny's. She must be very old now. She seemed old to me even when I was a child. I was always a little afraid of her. She was tall and thin and wore black all the time."

"Why do we have a drawer full of her stuff?" Katy asked.

Mrs. Turner was busy at the sink, scrubbing the racks from the oven. "Oh, she wanted Granny to store her things for her, but Granny has such a small apartment, and we have this big house. I said I'd take them. Aunt Martha put them away in the drawer herself. She told me to keep it locked. I thought she must have something very valuable there, but I peeked in the drawer. It's just some worn-out clothes. Old people are funny about those things."

Katy left the kitchen. She put on her coat and hat and went to see Louise. Louise was setting the table in her doll's house with the Mexican dishes. Katy told her what her mother had said about Aunt Martha.

"She sounds like a witch to me," said Louise.

"That's what I think too," Katy said. "It scares me."

"Why?" Louise started to rearrange the furniture in the doll's dining room.

"Don't you remember that everything we did with the gloves and the bathrobe caused trouble?" Katy said.

"Nothing terrible happened with the Seven League Boots," said Louise.

"It almost did — a couple of times. And now we can't use the boots because

we don't have a compass. Maybe Pilar
is in trouble."

Louise put down the little chair she
was holding. "Katy," she said, "have you
forgotten the magic mirror?"

The girls left Louise's apartment and
went to Katy's house. When they were
upstairs in Katy's room, Katy unlocked
the drawer. She sat on the floor, took
out the little mirror, and gazed into it.
"I wish I knew what Pilar was doing."

Louise leaned over Katy's shoulder to look in the mirror too. The surface of the glass flashed and changed color.

They were looking at Pilar's grandmother's stall in the market place. Pilar was talking to a man who was wearing a light summer suit. Katy saw that he was writing in a black notebook.

Today there were stacks of place mats in the stall and only a few baskets. Pilar's grandmother sat on a wooden chair weaving colored grass into a mat like the one Louise had made with the magic gloves.

Pilar seemed to be talking very slowly to the man. She kept shaking her head.

"Katy," Louise said. "I think Pilar is talking English. That man looks like an American. He seems to want to buy all her mats."

"And Pilar is asking him to pay more than he wants to," Katy said.

The girls had seen Pilar play this game

before. When the man shook his head and walked away they wondered if Pilar would run after him. Instead she sold a dozen mats to a red-haired lady who was wearing shorts and carrying a guitar, a rug, and a bunch of calla lilies.

A little later a young man and woman walked over to the stall. Pilar sold them a set of mats of different sizes. Then the man with the notebook came back and spoke to Pilar again. This time she nodded her head and smiled. The man wrote in his book. After that he took out a check book and made out a check which he gave to Pilar.

When the man had gone, Pilar gave the check to her grandmother. Then Pilar began to tie all the mats into bundles.

Katy put down the mirror. "I guess nothing awful is happening to Pilar after all. She certainly is good at the game of buying and selling."

CHAPTER FIFTEEN

Katy took the walnut wedding to school to show to the children in her class. She told them all about the Mexican market. "The people play a game every time they buy or sell anything," she said. "The game is for one person to see how much he can charge for something and for the other person to see how little he can pay for it."

"That's what is known as bargaining," Miss Johnson told the class.

The teacher was very pleased with Katy's talk. "I'm going to give you an *excellent* for it," she told her.

The walnut shell was passed around among the children. Each one had a good look at it. Richard Higgins offered to trade a Chinese puzzle for the walnut, but Katy wanted to keep the little wedding herself.

After school Richard walked behind Katy and Louise when they went home. He still wanted the walnut wedding.

"I'll give you twice what you paid for it," he said.

"I wouldn't take fifty times as much for it," Katy told him. "Go home, Richard." She turned to Louise. "Let's look in the mirror and see what Pilar is doing." She took the key to the drawer out of her coat pocket.

"First I have to go home to change my clothes," Louise said. "I'll come over to your house afterward."

Louise went into her apartment building. Richard caught up with Katy and walked beside her. "Come on," he said, "let me have the walnut."

"Why do you want it so much?" Katy asked him.

"Why do *you* want it, Katy?" Richard said.

Katy stopped walking and thought for a minute. "I'm not sure," she said. "I just do."

They were standing at the corner. Katy had one foot on the curbstone and one in the street.

"Let me see the walnut once more, Katy," Richard begged.

Katy took it out of her pocket. "Look, but don't touch," she said.

Richard made a grab for the walnut shell. Katy dodged him. The key fell out of her hand and down into the opening of a sewer.

"Now see what you made me do!" Katy cried. She put her books on the sidewalk and the walnut shell back into her pocket.

"What did you drop?" Richard asked.

"A key — an important key." Katy got down on her hands and knees and tried to reach into the sewer.

"What you need is a magnet and a string," Richard said.

"Where am I going to get them?" asked Katy.

"That's your problem. If you hadn't been so nasty about the walnut shell I might help you. Have fun." Richard crossed the street and walked down the block.

Louise was coming down the street. She was wearing blue jeans and a lumber jacket. "What's the matter, Katy? I thought you'd be home by now."

Katy picked up her books and stood up. She told Louise what had happened.

"I never did like Richard Higgins," Louise said. "But that was a good idea about the string and the magnet. There's a magnet sewn into the corner of one of my mother's potholders. See if you can get some string." She started back to her house.

Katy ran home. She changed her clothes and went down to the kitchen. She knew her mother kept pieces of string in the drawer of the cabinet.

Mrs. Turner was busy cutting up a chicken. "I'm going out for a little while, Mother," Katy said. She opened the drawer and found a long piece of string coiled around a pencil. Katy slipped the string off the pencil and put it into her pocket.

Mrs. Turner didn't look up. "Don't be out late," she said. "It gets dark early now."

Katy put on her jacket and went to join Louise. Her friend was waiting for her on the corner by the sewer opening. She handed Katy a square magnet.

"It's not very big," Katy said.

"It's all I've got. Do you have the string?" Louise tied the magnet to the string and the two girls got down on all fours in the gutter. Katy pushed the magnet into the sewer opening. Louise held the other end of the string and tried to swing the magnet back and forth. Then they carefully pulled it up again. Something was sticking to it. Katy looked to see what it was — a slimy nail.

The second try brought up two bobby pins, and on the third try the magnet slipped off the string and fell into the sewer. The string smelled like the sewer by this time. Katy and Louise decided to drop it into the sewer too.

"We'll look for a bigger magnet tomorrow," Katy said.

Louise stood up and stretched her legs. "There's no rush. Your mother seems to have forgotten all about that key."

CHAPTER SIXTEEN

It wasn't until she came home from school next day that Katy heard the bad news. She was sitting at the kitchen table eating graham crackers and drinking milk. Her mother came into the kitchen. "Look what came in the mail this morning, Katy."

"What is it?" Katy asked.

"An air mail letter from Aunt Martha." Mrs. Turner held up a sheet of blue paper. "It's funny that we were talking about her just the other day. And now she's coming here after all these years. She says she'll arrive tomorrow and take away the stuff from the drawer in your room. I'd better look for the key."

Suddenly the graham cracker tasted like dust in Katy's mouth. She felt as if she were going to choke. She swallowed the rest of her milk and went upstairs to her room.

Katy had been saving money to buy Christmas presents. She took a quarter out of her desk. She remembered seeing some large magnets in the Discount Center on Church Avenue.

There were only two magnets left in the store. Katy bought one of them. She took it with her to Louise's house. Louise was just getting ready to go to see Katy.

Katy showed her the magnet. "We don't have any time to lose. Aunt Martha is coming for her things tomorrow," she said. "Do you have any string?"

"I'll look." Louise searched the whole apartment. She finally took some string off a package of shirts her mother had just brought home from the laundry. "It's not very strong," she said. "Maybe we should braid it."

"We don't have time," Katy said, "and it would make the string too short. Come on."

The wind blew in gusts around the street corner where Katy had dropped the key. The girls got down on their hands and knees on the cold pavement and began to fish things out of the sewer. They brought up four bottle caps, a

twisted piece of wire, and the lid to a tin can — but no key.

"What a dirty place to play!" Old Mrs. Morris, Katy's next-door neighbor, was standing on the corner. "Get up from there this minute, Katy Turner. You know perfectly well your mother wouldn't want you doing that. You'll make yourself sick."

Katy stood up. Mrs. Morris walked away. "Busybody!" said Katy, under her breath.

Louise got to her feet. "My hands are freezing, and they smell terrible," she said. "Mr. Stern, the man in the hardware store, sells keys. He has a lot of them hanging on the peg board at the back of his store. Maybe there's one that will fit the drawer."

Katy was glad to have an excuse to stop fishing. Her hands were cold too. "I wonder how much a key would cost.

I still have some money."

They went to Katy's house to wash their hands.

"If we had the magic gloves," Katy said, "we could pick the lock of the drawer with a hairpin. But the gloves are in the drawer."

"Do you have a hairpin?" Louise asked.

"There might be one in my mother's room," said Katy.

Mrs. Turner was in her bedroom searching through all her drawers. She had emptied a lot of things onto the big double bed and was going through them. "Katy," she said, "have you seen a little key anywhere? I've lost the key to the storage chest."

Katy didn't want to answer. Instead she said, "I need a hairpin. Do you have one, Mother?"

"Take one off my dressing table," Mrs. Turner said. "Oh dear, Aunt Martha will be angry. Granny always said she had a terrible temper."

Katy took the hairpin and went back to her own room. "Louise," she whispered "my mother is looking for the key. She's afraid the witch will do something to her if she can't find it."

Louise took the hairpin and poked it into the lock of the drawer. She twisted it around. Nothing happened. "We'd better see if we can buy a key."

Katy took three quarters and four dimes out of her desk. "It's all I have," she said, "but I can't let the witch be angry with Mother. She might do something awful to her."

Church Avenue was crowded. Katy and Louise ran past three old ladies chatting before the shoemaker's shop. They dodged around the baskets of cucumbers and apples in front of the fruit stand. And they nearly bumped into a lady with a baby carriage. When they reached the hardware store they found Mr. Stern all alone at the back.

Katy was out of breath. She had to wait a minute before she could talk. Then she said, "I lost the key to a chest of drawers. I thought maybe you had one like it."

Mr. Stern reached up to a high shelf and took down a cardboard box. "Look in here," he said, "and see if you can spot anything that looks like it." He pointed to a pegboard. "There are more there."

Katy and Louise found three keys that looked as if they might fit the drawer. "I don't know which one to buy," Katy said. "I only have a dollar and fifteen cents."

"Tell you what you do," Mr. Stern said. "Take all three keys home with you and try them. Then you can come back and buy the one that fits. Just be sure you bring them back."

Katy thanked him and then she and Louise hurried home with the keys. It was beginning to get dark.

Two of the keys were too big for the keyhole. The third one went in easily. Katy held her breath. She turned the key. It slipped around in the keyhole, but it didn't open the lock.

"Let me try." Louise took the key out and blew on it. She wiggled it as she poked it into the keyhole. "I think I've got it," she said.

Still the key wouldn't unlock the drawer. Katy and Louise both tried several times. Then they gave up and took the keys back to Mr. Stern. After that Louise had to go home.

Katy had a sick feeling in her stomach. She could hardly eat her supper.

CHAPTER SEVENTEEN

Next morning Katy couldn't find her left shoe. She lay on her stomach and looked under the bed. Her shoe was wedged back in a corner against the wall. Right beside it Katy saw the metal box with the picture of the fruitcake on the lid. She had to move the bed to get them.

Then she picked up the box. It felt as if there were something inside it. Katy shook it. The box made a little clanking noise.

Suddenly Katy had a wild hope. She

was so excited that she could hardly open the box. It kept slipping out of her hands. Katy sat on the floor. She gripped the box between her knees to hold it steady and pried off the lid.

Katy looked into the box. There was the key she had dropped down the sewer. It still had a sewer smell. She was afraid she was dreaming. For a few moments Katy just sat and stared at it.

"Katy," she heard her mother call, "hurry. You'll be late for school."

Katy put on her other shoe, then she unlocked the bottom drawer of the chest and put away the box. She took the key downstairs to her mother. "Is this what you were looking for? I found it under my bed."

On the way to school Katy told Louise, "That fruitcake box seems to find things that are lost. We should have guessed it after we found my jacks and then your father's compass in it. We ought to have known *everything* in the drawer was magic."

"I could have used it last week," Louise said. "I got in awful trouble because I dropped one of the good spoons in the garbage, and it was thrown away."

After school, when Katy came home, her mother opened the front door for her. "Aunt Martha is here, Katy. She wants to meet you."

Katy walked into the living room. A very tall woman with white hair was standing by the piano. She was wearing a high-necked black lace blouse and a long black skirt. She turned and looked at Katy with sparkly green eyes.

"Your mother tells me you liked the rattle I gave you when you were a baby," she said. "I know someone who has a new baby girl. Do you think I should give her the rattle?"

"It was lost a long time ago," Katy said. Then she remembered the fruit-cake box. Would the rattle be in there if Aunt Martha was looking for it? she wondered.

Aloud Katy said, "Are you going to take away the things in the drawer, Aunt Martha?"

The old lady gave her a sharp look. "Yes," she said. "Did you have fun with them, Katy?"

Katy was taken by surprise. For a minute she didn't say anything. Then she grinned. "I sure did," she said. "Are you going to leave them in the house with the little girl who gets the rattle?"

Suddenly Aunt Martha smiled. "I might," she said.

END